For Marie
H. P.

For Siâny
E. S.

First published in the UK in 2020 by Nosy Crow Ltd
The Crow's Nest, 14 Baden Place, Crosby Row
London SE1 1YW, UK

Nosy Crow and associated logos are trademarks and/or registered
trademarks of Nosy Crow Ltd

Text copyright © Helen Peters, 2020
Cover and illustrations copyright © Ellie Snowdon, 2020

The right of Helen Peters and Ellie Snowdon to be identified
as the author and illustrator respectively of this work has been asserted
by them in accordance with the Copyright, Designs
and Patents Act 1988.

ISBN: 978 1 78800 832 7

A CIP catalogue record for this book will be available from the British Library.

Printed and bound in Great Britain by Clays Ltd, Elcograf S.p.A.

Papers used by Nosy Crow are made from wood grown in sustainable forests.

1 3 5 7 9 10 8 6 4 2
www.nosycrow.com

Chapter One
A Terrible Accident

"Good dog, Bramble," said Jasmine, as the spaniel came trotting back across the orchard with a battered tennis ball in her mouth. "Good dog."

Bramble dropped the soggy ball and Jasmine stroked her silky head. Then she picked up the ball and hurled it into the long grass.

"Fetch!" she called, and the spaniel wagged her tail and bounded after it. She was old now, but she still loved to play.

Bramble lived with Jasmine's pet pig, Truffle, in the big orchard at Oak Tree Farm. It was an

1

unusual friendship, but they had been friends ever since Jasmine had brought Truffle to the farm as a tiny runt. When Truffle was younger, she would chase balls too, but now she preferred to spend her days rooting around under the apple trees.

Jasmine's sheepdog, Sky, nuzzled into her knee. Jasmine looked down at the handsome black-and-white collie.

"Good boy, Sky," she said. "You're tired now, aren't you?"

She and Sky had just returned from a long walk in the woods. They didn't normally stay out this late, but it was a Friday and the beginning of the May half-term holiday, so Mum hadn't fussed about bedtime.

Sky licked Jasmine's hand and looked up at her adoringly. Jasmine ruffled the fur on the top of his head.

She had found Sky as an abandoned puppy, ill-treated and starving, and had nursed him back

2

to health. They had been devoted to each other from the moment they met, but it had taken a long time before Sky could really trust people again. He had bitten Jasmine once when he was frightened, and even now he sometimes got spooked by unfamiliar people and situations. But he was a very different dog from the frail and terrified puppy that Jasmine had scooped out of a hedge almost two years ago.

Jasmine looked up as car headlights appeared on the farm track.

"There you are," she said to Bramble. "Dad's back. You'll get your supper now."

Jasmine's dad was the farmer at Oak Tree Farm. He normally drove a truck, but he had used Jasmine's mum's car tonight to take her older sister Ella out to practise her driving. Ella had been having driving lessons for months, but she didn't seem to have made much progress.

"It will help her confidence if you take her out," Mum had said to Dad. "Bless her, she's

such a nervous driver. It will be good for her to practise in the evening too. She's only ever driven in daylight."

Jasmine noticed that her mum hadn't offered to take Ella herself. Ella was extremely clever and hardworking, but she was not a natural driver.

"If she could learn it all from a book, she'd be fine," Mum had said. "It's actually driving the car that's the problem."

"I can't wait to start driving lessons," Jasmine's little brother, Manu, had said. "I'll be the best driver ever."

Manu was staying at his best friend Ben's house tonight. Which was lucky, because otherwise he would have wanted to sit in the back of the car while Ella was driving. And Manu's comments were not the sort of thing a nervous driver needed to hear.

The car continued its jerky progress along the track. Jasmine smiled. "That's definitely Ella driving," she said to Sky.

Suddenly, the engine revved loudly. There was a horrible dull thud. Brakes screeched. Glass shattered.

Jasmine stood rooted to the spot. The engine stopped and she heard doors opening and then a terrifying high-pitched scream.

Jasmine unfroze. She raced out of the orchard and up the garden path. She burst through the back door of the farmhouse.

"Mum!" she yelled.

Her mum was reading at the kitchen table. She looked up as Jasmine ran into the room. Her eyes widened in alarm.

"What is it? Jasmine, what's wrong?"

"It's Ella," gasped Jasmine. "I think she's hurt."

Nadia sprang to her feet. "Where is she?"

"On the track. The car crashed and Ella was screaming."

But Nadia had already left the room. Jasmine sprinted up the farm track after her.

Dad was running towards them, his boots

pounding on the tarmac. In the beam of the headlights, Jasmine saw Ella kneeling in front of the car, her head in her hands, sobbing loudly, next to a brown mound of something Jasmine couldn't make out.

"Oh, thank goodness you're here," panted Dad.

"Is Ella OK?" cried Mum. "What happened?"

"Ella's fine," said Dad. "It's a deer. We hit a deer on the track."

Mum ran towards the car, Jasmine following her. She could see now that the brown mound was actually a beautiful deer, stretched out on its side with its eyes open in a fixed stare. Ella was hunched on her knees beside it, rocking to and fro with her head in her hands, wailing.

"Ella, are you OK?" asked Mum, crouching in front of her. "Were you hurt? Are you injured?"

"I'm a murderer," Ella wailed. "I've killed a deer."

"It wasn't your fault," said Dad. "Deer are really hard to avoid if they run across the road in

front of you. It was just a terrible accident."

"It *was* my fault," sobbed Ella. "If you'd been driving, she'd still be alive."

"I'm sure you did the best you could," said Mum.

"You don't understand," wailed Ella. "I'm completely stupid. I'm the stupidest person in the world."

Mum looked at Dad. "What actually happened?"

Dad sighed. "She panicked when she saw the deer. She tried to brake, but she pressed the accelerator instead."

Jasmine winced.

"I put the handbrake on, obviously," said Dad, "but by then we'd hit the deer."

Mum put her arm around Ella. "Sweetheart, I know you've had a horrible shock, but I need you to get up and move out of the way. I have to examine the deer. We don't want her to suffer any more than necessary, do we?"

8

Thank goodness Mum was a vet, Jasmine thought. She always knew what to do.

"You don't need to examine her," wailed Ella. "She's dead. I killed her."

Nadia sighed impatiently and stood up. "Michael, can you deal with her?" she said.

Dad crouched beside Ella and laid his hands on her shoulders. "Ella, you're in shock. I'm going to take you home. Mum will look after the deer. We're going to have to walk, because Mum might need the equipment in the car. Can you manage to walk?"

Still sobbing, Ella allowed Dad to help her to her feet.

"Right," said Mum. "Grab the torch from the glove compartment, please, Jasmine."

Dad put his arm around Ella and started to guide her down the track. When Jasmine returned with the torch, Nadia was holding her coat over the deer's head.

"Is she alive?" asked Jasmine.

"Only just, I think," said Mum. "I don't think she's going to make it."

Jasmine watched as Nadia lifted the coat from the deer's head.

"The reflex in the pupil of the eye is the last thing to work in a living animal," said Mum. "If the pupil size doesn't change when I shine a torch into her eye, then I'm afraid she's not alive."

She shone the torch beam straight into the doe's eye. Jasmine watched as the shiny black pupil contracted.

"She's alive!" she said.

"She is," said Nadia, "but barely. I don't want her to suffer any more."

She paused. Then she gave Jasmine a serious look and said, "There's something else, though. Something I didn't want to mention in front of Ella."

"What?" asked Jasmine.

But before Nadia could answer, Jasmine

saw something in the light of the torch beam. Something that made her gasp. A movement in the deer's stomach.

"Oh!" she exclaimed. "There's a baby inside her!"

Chapter Two

An Emergency Operation

"We're not going to be able to save the mother, I'm afraid," said Nadia, "but if we work very quickly there's a small chance that we could save the fawn."

She shone the torch beam into the doe's eye again. This time, the pupil didn't move.

"Oh, no," breathed Jasmine, and tears welled up in her eyes.

"Poor thing," said Nadia. "But at least she didn't suffer for too long. We need to work fast now. The fawn won't live inside the mother for

more than three or four minutes. Will you be my assistant?"

Jasmine's heart sped up. "Sure. What should I do?"

"Can you fetch my box of instruments? I'm going to need a scalpel blade. And a towel to dry the fawn as soon as it's born."

Jasmine hurried to the car boot and took out a clean towel and the big case containing Nadia's equipment. She set it on the ground beside her mum and opened the lid.

Nadia pulled on a pair of disposable gloves and unwrapped a gleaming scalpel blade from its sterile packaging.

"Normally I'd shave the animal's hair around the area where I'm going to operate," she said, "but in this case we don't need to worry too much about hygiene. The only thing that matters is getting the little one out as quickly as possible. Can you hold the torch steady while I operate? It's lucky you're not squeamish."

13

She inserted the scalpel blade into a handle and poised the blade above the deer's stomach. "When I take the fawn out, you hold its back legs firmly and pull, while I help the rest of it out."

"OK," said Jasmine. She held the torch so its beam shone on the deer's stomach. The mother's reddish-brown coat rippled and bulged as the fawn moved inside her.

"Ready?" asked Nadia.

"Ready," said Jasmine.

It all happened very quickly. Jasmine watched, fascinated, as Nadia pulled out a tiny pair of hooves, followed by the fawn's skinny little back legs.

"Keep a tight hold of the legs," she said, "and pull on them steadily. Careful, they're slippery."

Jasmine put the torch down, took hold of the wet slippery legs and pulled, as Nadia eased the rest of the fawn out.

"Oh, it's gorgeous!" said Jasmine, as a perfect

little head appeared. "It's so tiny!"

"She," corrected Nadia. "Look, she's a doe."

"She's so still," said Jasmine. "Is she alive?"

"She's not breathing," said Nadia. "Hold her upside down and I'll compress her chest."

Jasmine dangled the little creature upside down by her back legs, while Nadia worked furiously on the chest.

"Normally the chest would be compressed as the animal's being born," she said, "but that doesn't happen if it's born by caesarean, so you have to do it manually."

The fawn made no sound or movement. Nadia leaned over and picked one of the long tough grass stems that grew by the side of the track. She tickled the fawn's nostrils with it.

Suddenly, the fawn gave a spluttery cough. Jasmine laughed in delight. "She's alive!"

The fawn gasped for air.

"She's starting to breathe," said Nadia, still working on her chest. "That's right, little one.

Keep breathing."

The fawn spluttered and coughed again. Then she shook her tiny head. Nadia smiled. "That's what we want to see." She handed the towel to Jasmine. "Wrap her in this and rub her dry. We need to warm her up and make sure her circulation's working."

Jasmine wrapped the little fawn in the towel and started to dry her, first her tummy and legs, and then her head and face.

"She's got such big ears," said Jasmine. "And such gorgeous dark eyes. I can't believe how small she is. Should she be this small?"

"I'm not sure,"

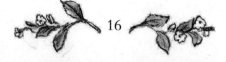

said Nadia, "but roe deer are the smallest of all the native deer. She's absolutely tiny, isn't she? I could almost fit her in the palm of my hand."

"Tiny but perfect," said Jasmine.

The fawn shook her head again. Then she kicked out her back legs and wriggled.

"Look, she's getting really lively," said Jasmine. "She's going to be fine, isn't she?"

"It's impossible to tell," said Nadia. "The first few days will be crucial."

"I'll spend all my time with her," said Jasmine. "I'll be her foster mother."

"That's exactly what she needs," said Nadia. "You have to bond with fawns immediately if they're going to survive. It's lucky it's your half term. She's going to need you to do everything for her."

Jasmine helped Nadia move the poor mother deer to the side of the track, and then they drove back to the farmyard. Jasmine held the fawn on

her lap, wrapped in a dry towel, talking to her
softly.

"I want her to get used to the sound of my
voice," she said. "Then she'll recognise me as her
mother."

Dad was making a cup of tea in the kitchen as
Mum walked in ahead of Jasmine.

"Where's Ella?" asked Mum.

"I made her go to bed," said Dad. "She's in a
pretty bad way, poor thing."

"I'll go up and see her as soon as I've washed
my hands," said Mum. "Remember to give yours
a good scrub too, Jasmine. And would you mind
taking the truck to collect the deer, Michael?"

"Sure," said Dad. "Poor Ella. I don't think
she'll be getting back behind the wheel any time
soon."

Nadia left the room and Dad turned to
Jasmine, standing in the doorway with the
bundled-up towel in her arms.

"What have you got there?" he asked.

18

Jasmine smiled and walked towards him. Dad stared in surprise.

"She had a fawn?"

"She was pregnant," said Jasmine. "Mum did an emergency caesarean. It was amazing." She stroked the fawn's soft ears. "She's a girl."

"Wow," said Dad. "So now you have an orphaned fawn to rear. That's going to be a lot of work."

Jasmine smiled. "I know."

Dad stroked the fawn's head. "You'd better pop her in the Aga while you get things ready."

He opened the bottom door of the big Aga cooker and laid a sheet of newspaper on the oven floor.

Visitors to the farm in springtime, seeing the oven door open, were sometimes alarmed at the sight of a tiny live lamb lying in the Aga. The family would have to reassure them that the animal wasn't being cooked for dinner. In fact, the bottom oven produced a very gentle heat that was exactly the right temperature for warming up sick or motherless baby animals that needed a bit of extra care.

"Once she's warmed up, you can bring in the puppy crate for her," said Dad.

"We'd better keep the cats out of the kitchen," said Jasmine. "They're bigger than her."

Jasmine had two cats. Toffee was a ginger tom and Marmite had pure-black fur and amber

20

eyes. They were normally calm and gentle, but
Jasmine didn't want to take any chances.

"She'll need colostrum, won't she?" Jasmine
said. "Should I use the same formula we use for
the lambs?"

"Yes, that should be fine," said Dad. "Well,
it'll have to be, since we don't have any deer
colostrum."

Colostrum was the mother's first milk, and a
baby animal couldn't survive without it. It was a
special type of milk that contained extra protein
and also antibodies to protect the newborn
animal from diseases. Because this fawn was an
orphan who couldn't feed from her mother, she
would need a powdered colostrum substitute.

Jasmine carefully unwrapped the fawn from
the towel. She smiled in delight as she saw her
properly for the first time. Outside on the track,
it had been too dark and the situation had been
too urgent to notice any details.

"Look how beautiful she is!" exclaimed

Jasmine. "Look at her eyes! And hasn't she got the most gorgeous coat?"

The little deer was incredibly beautiful. She had huge dark almond-shaped eyes in a delicate face, with a shiny black nose and large fluffy ears. Her neck and legs were covered in light-brown fur and her back was dark brown with wobbly rows of white spots.

"She looks like someone's dotted white paint all along her back," said Jasmine. "I'm going to call her Dotty."

"Dotty the deer," said Dad. "Nice."

Dotty's eyes were fixed on Jasmine. She put out her little pink tongue and licked Jasmine's hand.

"Look!" exclaimed Jasmine. "She likes me!"

She kissed the little deer on the top of her furry brown head and gently laid her in the bottom oven.

"You rest there," she said, "and I'll get your colostrum ready."

She put the kettle on and went out to the scullery, where Dad kept the bottle-feeding equipment for the lambs. From the cupboard under the sink, she fetched a bottle, a rubber teat, a sachet of colostrum formula and a small whisk.

While she was whisking the powder into the boiled water, Dad went to the garage to fetch Sky's puppy crate.

"Maybe seeing the fawn will make Ella feel a bit better," he said when he returned.

"It might make her feel worse," said Jasmine. "Knowing that Dotty's an orphan because of her."

Dad sighed as he set the crate down beside the Aga. "You may be right. Poor Ella. It's my fault. I shouldn't have let her drive in the dark."

A scuffling noise came from the oven. Jasmine looked round.

"Oh, look! Dotty's trying to stand up."

The little fawn lifted her head. Her tiny hooves scrabbled on the newspaper as she struggled to get a foothold on the slippery surface. She jerked

23

her back up a few centimetres and then slumped down again.

"Shall I help her?" asked Jasmine.

"No, leave her be," said Dad. "She's finding her strength. She needs to do it herself."

Nadia came into the kitchen, carrying the bathroom scales in one hand and her laptop in the other.

"How's Ella?" asked Dad.

"Not great. It's terrible timing too, in the middle of her A levels. I hope she gets some sleep."

Dad sighed again and took his truck keys from the hook on the wall. "I'll go and collect the deer now, before I check the sheep."

"Thanks, Michael," said Mum, as he left the kitchen.

"Are those scales for weighing Dotty?" asked Jasmine.

Nadia smiled. "Dotty, is it? That's a sweet name."

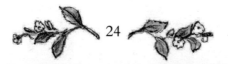

24

As if she knew they were talking about her, Dotty started frantically scuffling around in the oven. She kicked with her front legs until they dangled out of the oven door. She planted her tiny front hooves on the kitchen tiles and heaved herself into a sitting position, looking out at them.

"Oh, she's so pretty!" said Nadia. "Look at that gorgeous little face. I hope we can keep her."

Jasmine frowned. "You can't give her away. You said I could look after her."

"That's not what I meant," said Mum. She gave Jasmine a serious look. "It's just that roe deer fawns are very difficult to look after. People say they're one of the hardest wild animals to hand-rear if they're orphaned. We'll do our very best, but you'll need to be prepared for the fact that she might not survive. And if she doesn't, you absolutely mustn't blame yourself. Promise me that."

Chapter Three
She's Very Independent

Jasmine gazed at the beautiful little fawn. What was Mum talking about?

"There's nothing wrong with her," she said. "She's perfect. And she's already trying to stand up."

"She looks great," said Mum, "but it can be very hard to get them to feed, apparently. They don't always take to a bottle."

"I'm sure she'll let me feed her," said Jasmine. "I'll try now."

"Let's just weigh her first," said Mum, setting

the scales on the floor.

Jasmine took a notepad and pen from the drawer to write down Dotty's weight. It was important to weigh baby animals every day when you were hand-rearing them. It was the only way to tell whether they were eating enough and growing properly.

"How much should she weigh?" she asked.

"I'm not sure, to be honest," said Mum. "We can look it up."

"I wish Tom was here," said Jasmine. "Can I phone him?"

Mum laughed. "It's too late to phone now. Wait until morning."

"I can't wait to tell him," said Jasmine. "He'll be so excited."

Tom was Jasmine's best friend, and they were planning to run an animal rescue centre when they grew up. They had already rescued several animals. But Tom was away this weekend, so he would have to wait to meet Dotty.

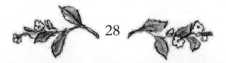

Dotty kicked out her back legs and pushed herself forward. She shook her head and heaved her way out of the oven. As her back legs emerged, her front legs wobbled and she flopped to her knees on the tiles.

Jasmine knelt in front of the Aga. "Come on, Dotty," she whispered. "You can do it."

The little deer stretched out her neck and licked Jasmine's hand.

"Oh, she's bonded with you already," said Nadia. "That's wonderful."

Dotty wobbled to her feet again, with her front legs crossed over each other and her back legs splayed wide apart. Jasmine held her breath as the fawn carefully uncrossed her front legs until they were planted in the right position, underneath her shoulders. She swayed from side to side. Then she collapsed on to her knees again.

"It looks like such hard work for her," said Jasmine.

"It's amazing, though, isn't it?" said Mum.

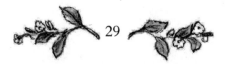

29

"It takes human babies a year to stand up, yet
animals can do it in less than an hour. Right, let's
get her on the scales, and then you can try her
with that colostrum."

They sat her on the scales. "One point eight
kilograms," said Jasmine. "That's nothing!"

"Half the size of you when you were born,"
said Nadia.

"When I've fed her, I'll make a proper chart,
with her weight and the amount she drinks at
every feed," Jasmine said. "And then I'm going to
look up everything about roe deer fawns."

Nadia smiled. "You might want to get some
sleep at some point too."

"It's half term," said Jasmine. "I can sleep any
time."

She lifted Dotty off the scales and gently
lowered her to the ground. Dotty immediately
began scrabbling to her feet again.

"She's very independent," said Jasmine
approvingly. "She's determined to stand on

her own."

As if to prove Jasmine's point, Dotty carefully planted her feet apart to balance herself. And there she stood, wobbly but upright, looking up at her foster mother.

"Well done, Dotty!" said Jasmine, bending down to stroke the little fawn. "Look, Mum, she's properly standing."

"That's great," said Nadia. "A very good sign."

Jasmine fetched the bottle. "Now, here's some lovely warm colostrum. This will make you really strong."

She pulled up her sleeve and shook a little of the colostrum on to her wrist to test the temperature. The milk felt the same temperature as her skin, which meant it was just right.

She turned to her mother. "Should I sit her on my lap to feed her?"

"No, fawns should always be fed standing up," Nadia said.

"Well, it's lucky you're standing then, Dotty,"

said Jasmine.

"Hold the bottle at an angle and keep it above her, so she has to stretch her neck and head to feed," said Mum. "It might not look comfortable, but it's how they feed in the wild."

Dotty was so tiny that her head only came up to Jasmine's knee. Jasmine crouched in front of her and held the teat just above her mouth, but Dotty turned away. Jasmine held her head gently with one hand and squeezed the teat until a few drops of colostrum dribbled out on to Dotty's lips.

This trick usually worked with lambs. A little taste would encourage the animal to open its mouth, and then you could slip the teat in and with any luck they would start to suck.

It didn't work with Dotty, though. Her mouth stayed firmly shut.

"Come on, Dotty," said Jasmine. She dribbled a bit more colostrum between Dotty's lips but the fawn jerked her head away again. Jasmine

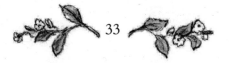

gently pulled her lips apart but Dotty wouldn't open her mouth. Using a bit more force, Jasmine opened it enough to slip the whole teat in. But Dotty just spat it out.

Mum's phone rang and she went into the other room to answer it. Jasmine kept talking softly and stroking the little deer as she tried to encourage her to drink in every way she knew. But Dotty seemed completely uninterested. Eventually, she swayed and sank to her knees again.

"Oh, Dotty," sighed Jasmine.

The kitchen door opened and Dad appeared with a sack full of hay. "There you go," he said, stuffing hay into the crate. "That should keep her comfortable."

"She's refusing to suck," Jasmine said. "Even if I get the teat into her mouth, she just spits it out again."

"Give her time," said Dad. "You can try again in a while. Just wipe that milk from around her mouth. Don't want her getting sore." He went back out to the lambing barn.

Jasmine found a cloth in the scullery, where Mum kept a bag of old clothes to use as rags. She dampened the cloth with warm water and wiped the milk from Dotty's face. Dotty seemed to like having her face washed. She licked Jasmine's hand again. Jasmine stroked her big soft ears. "You're so lovely," she murmured. "But you need to drink your milk, OK?"

Mum came back into the kitchen, holding her phone.

35

"I'm really sorry," she said, "but I've got to go out. That was Matthew Evans on the phone. His dog's very ill and he thinks she might have picked up some poison. Dad will be in the lambing barn if you need him."

Jasmine's worry must have shown on her face, because Mum said, "Why don't you phone Mira? She'll be able to give you some advice."

Mira was Mum's friend at the Wildlife Trust. She had helped Jasmine and Tom when they had rescued an otter cub the previous summer.

"Isn't it a bit late to phone her?" asked Jasmine.

Mum laughed. "No, she'll still be up, don't worry about that."

"Can you call her?" asked Jasmine. She wasn't keen on phoning people she didn't know well.

"I would," said Mum, "but I have to go. Just give her a call. She'll be delighted to hear from you. And I'll be back as soon as I can."

Chapter Four
Babies are Easier than Fawns

The pinboard on the kitchen wall was a jumble of photos, messages, school letters and emergency phone numbers. Jasmine found Mira's name and number scrawled on the back of an old receipt. With a tight feeling in her stomach, she picked up the phone.

To her relief, Mira sounded pleased to hear from her.

"I'm sorry it's so late," Jasmine said. "But it's an emergency." And she explained the situation as briefly as she could.

"Have you tried a syringe?" asked Mira.

"Not yet."

"Well, that's what I'd do. Feed her with a one-mil syringe for as long as it takes. Some fawns will start sucking on it very quickly, and some take ages. They're all different. But once she starts to suck on the syringe, you can switch to a bottle."

"How much should I give her?" asked Jasmine.

"Ten millilitres every two hours, in one-mil shots. She might try to spit the syringe out, so put it in the corner of her mouth. That way the milk's more likely to go down her throat."

"Is that just in the daytime, or during the night as well?" asked Jasmine.

"All through the night too, I'm afraid," said Mira. "After about a week, you can increase the amount and reduce the feeds to every three hours, and then to every four hours, and so on as she gets older."

"What if she won't feed from a syringe either?"

"Then you'll have to tube-feed her. But I'd leave that as a last resort."

"OK," said Jasmine. "Thank you so much, Mira."

"You're going to be exhausted, I'm afraid," said Mira. "Orphaned fawns need so much from you. They have to bond with just one person, so you're going to have to do all her feeds yourself. And she'll be permanently attached to your knee, like a shadow. You won't even be able to go to the toilet without her standing outside the door squeaking. I've got two children and, I can tell you now, babies are easier than fawns."

"Fawns are much cuter, though," said Jasmine, and Mira laughed.

"What about the dogs?" Jasmine asked. "Will they get on together?"

"I'd try to keep them apart as much as possible," said Mira. "They should be fine with her, but it wouldn't be good for her to get too friendly with them. A lot of young deer are

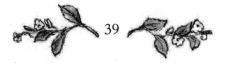

killed by dogs, so you don't want her running up to strange dogs once she's back in the wild."

"No," said Jasmine. "Definitely not."

But that wasn't going to be easy, she thought. If Dotty needed to be with her the whole time, when would she be able to walk Sky?

She said goodbye to Mira and fetched a one-mil syringe from the animal medicine cupboard. Then she sat down with the laptop to find out more about roe deer while Dotty slept.

Half an hour later, a rustling sound came from the puppy crate. Dotty raised her head and looked around enquiringly. Jasmine crouched in front of her.

"Hello, Dotty," she said, opening the door and stroking her. "Did you have a nice snooze?"

Dotty scuffled her twig-thin legs about in the hay, trying to get to her feet.

"Good girl," said Jasmine, kissing the top of her head. "You stand up, and then I can feed you."

She boiled the kettle, poured the hot water

40

into a jug and stood the feeding bottle in it to warm up the colostrum.

As if she understood what was needed, Dotty shakily got to her feet. She daintily uncrossed her tiny front hooves and planted them beneath her shoulders.

"Well done, Dotty," said Jasmine. "I'm going to feed you with a syringe now. I'll drop the milk

in the corner of your mouth, so you won't have to suck."

She laid some sheets of newspaper on the floor to catch any mess. She had discovered from her reading that mother deer lick their babies' bottoms during or after feeding, to encourage their toileting. Newborn fawns need this help from their mothers for a couple of weeks, until they learn to do it by themselves.

Jasmine wasn't planning to go that far, obviously, so she followed the advice she had read and dampened a piece of kitchen towel to wipe Dotty with instead. Then she lifted Dotty out of the crate and set her down on the newspaper. Dotty swayed slightly but she stayed upright.

Jasmine gave the bottle a good shake, pinching the teat so the milk didn't leak out. Then she tested the temperature on her wrist again.

"Perfect," she said. "Now you can have a lovely drink."

She unscrewed the top of the bottle, dipped the tiny syringe into the colostrum and drew up a millilitre of the thick yellowy liquid.

"Please don't spit the syringe out, Dotty. You really need this food."

Holding Dotty's face with one hand, she inserted the plastic nozzle into the corner of the fawn's mouth and quickly pushed the plunger before Dotty could protest. Then she withdrew the nozzle and watched.

And, to her joy, she saw the little deer swallow!

"Finally!" whispered Jasmine, with a sigh of relief. "Well done, Dotty. Just nine more to go."

It took ages, but finally Dotty had swallowed ten millilitres of liquid in one-millilitre shots. As she swallowed the last drop, Jasmine suddenly felt exhausted.

"Two hours until your next feed," she said. "Time for sleep."

Her legs were stiff as she got to her feet. She fetched the puppy crate to take it to her room. Then she turned to tell Dotty she would come back to fetch her. But Dotty wasn't there.

Jasmine frowned in puzzlement.

"Dotty?"

A little wet tongue licked her hand. Jasmine looked down and there was Dotty, standing at her knee, gazing up at her adoringly.

"Oh, you're following me around already! Clever girl. I'm not sure you're going to be able to walk upstairs, though. Come on."

And she tucked the fawn into the crook of her arm and made her way to bed.

Chapter Five
A Crazy Idea

Nadia looked up as Jasmine walked into the kitchen the following morning, cradling Dotty in her arms.

"Oh, well done, Jasmine," she said. "So you got her to feed."

"I used a syringe," said Jasmine, and she told Nadia about Mira's advice and the two-hourly feeds all through the night.

"You must be exhausted," said Nadia. "Why don't you go back to bed and let me do the next feed?"

Jasmine shook her head. "Roe deer fawns will only feed from one person."

Mum raised her eyebrows. "Well, in that case, I think you might be in for a very tiring half term."

"It's OK," said Jasmine. "I'll sleep when she sleeps, in between her feeds."

"And what about your other animals?" said Nadia. "Who's going to look after them?"

Just then, Ella walked in. Her eyes widened in delight as she saw the little fawn. "Oh my goodness!" she exclaimed. "Where did it come from?"

Then her look changed to one of horror. She clapped her hands over her mouth.

"Oh, no! Is this… Is she…? Oh, I killed her mother, didn't I!"

She dashed out of the room, ran upstairs and slammed her bedroom door shut.

Nadia sighed. "I'll go up and see her."

While Jasmine knelt on the kitchen floor

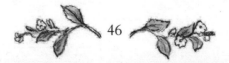

46

feeding Dotty and talking to her encouragingly,
she was also thinking. By the time Dotty had
finished, Jasmine had a plan. She scooped the
tiny deer into her arms and carried her up to
Ella's room.

Ella was curled up on her bed, sobbing. Mum
was sitting beside her, trying to comfort her.

"It was an accident," Mum was saying. "And
we managed to save the fawn."

"I made her an orphan," sobbed Ella. "She'd
be out in the wild with her mother if it wasn't
for me. I've ruined her life."

"You haven't ruined her life," said Nadia. "She's
got Jasmine to look after her. Any animal that has
Jasmine to look after it is very lucky."

Jasmine walked over to Ella. Nadia shifted
along so she could sit next to her sister.

"She's called Dotty," said Jasmine. "Look at her,
Ella."

Ella shook her head. She was still curled up in
a ball.

"I'll do everything I can to be as good a
mother as her real mother would have been,"
said Jasmine. "And when she's grown-up she'll
go back into the wild. So she'll have just as good
a life."

"But she won't have a mother," said Ella, in a
muffled, choked voice.

"I'm her mother now," said Jasmine. "I've been
with her since she was born and she's imprinted
on me. I'll do everything her real mother
would."

"But you've got all your other animals to look after."

"Yes," said Jasmine. "I was thinking about that." She paused, avoiding eye contact with her mum. Nadia would think this was a crazy idea.

"I'm going to have to be with Dotty all the time this week," she said. "And Mira said I should keep her away from dogs. So I was wondering if you might be able to help out with my other animals."

Ella finally took her head out of her hands. She gave Jasmine a startled stare.

"Me?"

"Yes, why not? It's only walking Sky, and feeding and mucking out Truffle. I know you're revising for your exams, but you need a break sometimes, and Mum always says it's good to get fresh air and exercise."

She risked a glance at Nadia. As she had predicted, Nadia was gazing at her as though she had completely lost her mind. Ella was most

definitely an indoor person, happiest when absorbed in a book or writing an essay. She was not somebody who mucked out pigs or took sheepdogs for walks.

Jasmine shrugged. "It was just an idea. If you wanted to do something to help."

Ella finally allowed her gaze to settle on the beautiful little fawn. Dotty gazed serenely back at her. Ella's face, which had been screwed tight with misery, relaxed slightly.

"All right," she said.

Nadia's eyebrows shot up in amazement.

"Really?" said Jasmine. "Mucking out Truffle and everything?"

"I need to do something to help," said Ella, "since this is all my fault. And I've been thinking I should get outside and do a bit of exercise this half term."

"Oh, that's great!" said Jasmine. "Thank you so much."

"What about when you go back to school,

though?" asked Ella. "Won't Dotty still need you around all the time?"

Jasmine shrugged. She had already started thinking about that too.

"Don't worry," she said. "I'll work something out."

When Jasmine sat down for breakfast, her eyelids felt so heavy she could hardly stay awake. So after breakfast she carried Dotty into the living room and lay on the sofa with the fawn nestled in her arms, where they both immediately fell into a deep, blissful sleep.

Jasmine was woken by a high-pitched squeaking sound. Before she could even open her eyes, she felt a wet tongue on her cheek. She sat up, laughing as she wiped her face with her sleeve.

"Hello, Dotty," she said. "Are you hungry again?"

She set Dotty on the floor, where she stood, wobbling on her stick-thin legs. Jasmine looked at the clock.

"Nearly eleven. Let's get you some food."

Dotty followed her to the kitchen, her head brushing Jasmine's knee. She stood beside her while she made up the colostrum formula. Then she trotted across the room with her when Jasmine fetched a sheet of newspaper and spread it on the floor.

"Wow," said Jasmine. "You really do follow your mum everywhere, don't you? I guess that makes sense if you're living in the wild."

She looked at the tiny, wobbly-legged animal.

Dotty would have no chance against a dog or a fox. She would need her mum's protection the whole time. So it was her instinct to stay constantly at her mother's side.

Jasmine told Tom all about it on the phone later that day.

"How will she be able to live in the wild when she's an adult, though," asked Tom, "if she's imprinted on you?"

When they had rescued Pebble the otter and Star the barn owl, they had to be really careful not to handle them too much, because if they imprinted on humans, they would never be properly wild again.

"Deer aren't like a lot of other wild animals," said Jasmine. "I was reading about it. They have to bond with one carer, but they can still go and live successfully in the wild once they're adults."

"Wow, that's perfect," said Tom. "I can't wait to see her. Can I come round as soon as we get home?"

"Of course," said Jasmine. "You won't believe how amazing she is."

For some reason, though, she didn't tell Tom her one big worry. The first few days were crucial. Dotty had to learn how to suck from a teat. But first she had to start sucking from the syringe, and she still showed no interest in this at all.

Jasmine was preparing Dotty's four o'clock feed in the kitchen when she heard the back door open. Her mum had been to fetch her little brother Manu from his first day at a half-term football camp.

"Take your boots off, Manu, and go and have a shower," Mum said, sounding very stressed. "Honestly, I'm so cross with you. I've never been so embarrassed in my entire life."

"I don't know why you're mad," said Manu. "I didn't do anything."

"Don't make me even crosser," said Mum. "I'm going to get the shopping from the car."

55

Manu walked into the kitchen. Every part of him, from his hair down to his socks, was coated in mud. His eyes widened as he saw Dotty. "Oh, he's so cute! Where did you get him?"

"She's a girl," said Jasmine. "Her mum was killed in a car accident."

She didn't mention exactly how Dotty's mother had been killed. The last thing Ella needed at the moment was endless questions and comments from her brother.

"Can I feed her?" asked Manu.

"No," said Jasmine. "She has to have just one carer, and that's me."

"That's not fair," said Manu. "I bet she'd like me to feed her."

"Why's Mum so mad at you?" asked Jasmine. "What did you do?"

"I didn't do anything," said Manu. "Me and Ben were just putting different things in our sandwiches, that's all."

"What sort of things?"

"Just normal things. We took the cheese out and put in grass and leaves and stuff. Just to see what they tasted like in a sandwich."

"But why's Mum so mad?" asked Jasmine, as she filled the syringe with colostrum. Eating grass and leaves was fairly normal behaviour for Manu, and Mum was usually quite relaxed about that sort of thing.

Manu shrugged. "How should I know?"

Nadia appeared in the doorway with two bags of shopping. She glared at Manu.

"Really? You don't know why I was mad? Daring everybody to eat soil, and making that

57

little boy so sick that his mother had to come
and take him home?"

"He was just making a fuss," protested Manu.
"I've ate worms before and I wasn't sick."

"Worms?" said Jasmine. "You said grass and
leaves."

Manu grinned. "We just put a little tasty worm
in his one, to see if he'd notice."

"That's not very nice," said Jasmine. "For the
boy or the worm."

"It's fine for the worm," said Manu. "Ollie
only ate half of it and then he spat it out. And
worms grow back again if they're cut in half."

"I don't want to hear another word," said
Mum. "Go and have your shower. I need to look
at a calf Dad's worried about."

Jasmine had been too distracted to focus
completely on Dotty, so when the syringe was
jerked out of her hand, it took her a couple
of seconds to register what was happening.
She took hold of the syringe again but Dotty

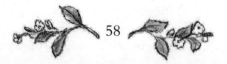

58

clamped her lips around it and pulled.

"Oh, Dotty!" said Jasmine, her face breaking into a huge smile. "You're sucking! Well done! Oh, my goodness. Right, wait there."

She took the syringe out of Dotty's mouth and fetched the feeding bottle. She screwed the teat on and offered it to the fawn.

"Here you are," she said. "Now you can suck properly."

But Dotty didn't open her mouth. Jasmine remembered Mira's advice. She pushed her finger into the left side of Dotty's mouth and slipped the teat in. Still Dotty didn't suck, so Jasmine gently moved the teat backwards and forwards to encourage her. Almost immediately, she felt a pull. She held the bottle firmly, silently willing Dotty to continue.

And Dotty did. She sucked until all the colostrum had disappeared. Even then, she continued to suck on air until Jasmine pulled the teat from her mouth.

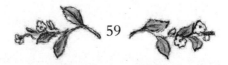

"Well done, Dotty!" she said, wrapping her arms around the fawn and kissing the top of her head. "You've done it!"

Chapter Six

Do We Have to Release Her?

For three days, Dotty stayed in the house, following Jasmine between the kitchen and the living room, feeding every two hours and sleeping in Jasmine's room at night. On the fourth morning, Jasmine said, "I think she's ready to go into the garden."

Her heart swelled with pride as she fastened Sky's old puppy collar around Dotty's neck and attached a little lead. A few days ago, she would never have imagined she would be taking her very own fawn for a walk.

Dotty stopped every few
steps to investigate a leaf, a twig or a
flower. It was the slowest walk ever, but
Jasmine loved it. She felt as though she was
experiencing the world for the first time,
through Dotty's eyes.

"In a few more days you'll be eating
those plants as well as sniffing
them," she said.

"I will not be eating daisies,"
said a voice behind her.

Jasmine turned. "Tom! Did you
just get back?"

"She's so tiny!" Tom said. "I didn't
know fawns were that small."

"I'm getting her used to going
outside," said Jasmine. "She'll start
nibbling earth soon."

"Nibbling earth? Why?"

"They get minerals from it, apparently. Maybe that's what Manu was trying to do when he made his soil sandwiches."

As they walked around the garden, Jasmine told Tom all she had learned about roe deer.

"What about when school starts?" asked Tom, as they finally walked back towards the house. "Will she still need feeding every two hours?"

"Every three hours next week," said Jasmine. "So I can feed her at six in the morning, and then if I go to school in the car instead of walking, I can feed her again just before nine. So then the next one would be at twelve." She looked at Tom. "Will you help me write a really polite email to the school? I need to get permission to come home at lunchtimes next week."

"Look," said Tom, pointing at a small black object hovering in the sky. "Who's flying a drone over your farm?"

"Some guy who lives in the village," said Jasmine. "Dad said he could come up here and fly it."

But Tom wasn't looking at the drone any more. He was staring over the hedge into the farmyard, his eyes huge with amazement.

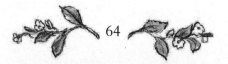

"That's not Ella?" he said. "Pushing a
wheelbarrow? No way."

Ella wheeled the barrow to the garden gate.
Sky was at her side, wagging his tail.

"Hi, Tom," she said. "How are you?"

Tom appeared to have been struck dumb.

Jasmine hastily scooped Dotty into her arms as Sky ran to greet her. She passed the fawn to Tom before she bent down to stroke her dog.

"Good boy," she said. "Did you behave yourself with Ella?"

"He was good as gold," said Ella. "Sometimes he runs off to investigate things, but he always comes back when I call him."

"Don't let him go too far away," said Jasmine. "He can get a taste for freedom, and then he won't come back when you call."

"He'll be fine," said Ella. "He likes me, don't you, Sky?"

Tom finally found his voice. "Have you been mucking out Truffle?" he asked.

Ella smiled at him. "Don't sound so surprised. I'm just helping Jasmine with her animals while she's looking after Dotty."

"Ella actually likes mucking out Truffle, don't you?" said Jasmine.

"Not so much the actual mucking out," said

Ella, "but it's very
satisfying when she
wriggles around
in the fresh straw
making all those
happy grunting
noises."

Nadia was on the
phone as they walked
into the kitchen. She did
not sound happy.

"I'm *so* sorry," she was saying. "Honestly, I
don't know what's got into them. First the
sandwiches and now this. I'm *so* sorry."

Jasmine raised her eyebrows at Tom. "Manu
and Ben," she whispered. "They're at football
camp."

"Yes, please do cut them," said Mum to the
person on the phone.

Jasmine stared at her. Cut what?

"Yes, I'm sure Ben's mum would give

67

permission," said Mum. "I've got some spares at home. I'll bring them over now."

She put the phone down and sank on to a chair, propping her head in her hands.

"What's happened?" asked Jasmine.

Mum raised her head and stared blankly at the kitchen wall for a few seconds before sighing heavily.

"Shoelaces," she said.

"Shoelaces?"

"Manu and Ben held a knot-tying competition during the lunch break. They encouraged a whole group of boys to take the laces out of their football boots, and then they all tied each other's ankles together. So now there's about six boys who can't play football because nobody can untie the knots. And I need to go and deliver spare shoelaces to the football field."

She sighed again as she got up. "If only Ella could drive, I could have got her to do it, and I'd have been spared the embarrassment."

"You should be used to it by now," said
Jasmine.

"I suppose I should," said Nadia. "But I don't
think I ever will be."

Jasmine's head teacher was surprisingly
reasonable about her request. It was arranged
that Dad would collect Jasmine from school at
lunchtime every day the following week and
bring her back in time for afternoon lessons.

"Bella's going to be so mad," said Tom.

Bella Bradley was in Jasmine and Tom's class,
and she was their worst enemy. Two years ago,
her dog had killed a nesting duck beside the
river while Jasmine and Tom had tried in vain
to stop it. Jasmine might just about have been
able to forgive Bella if she had been sorry, but all
Bella had said was, "So? It's just a duck."

Tom was right. Bella was mad. She always
hated it when anyone got more attention than
she did.

"I don't see why *she* gets special permission to go home at lunchtimes," she said loudly at morning break on their first day back. "Someone else could easily feed that deer."

"Actually, roe deer fawns need just one person looking after them," said Jasmine. "Or else they die. But you wouldn't care about that, would you?"

That shut Bella up. For the moment, anyway.

Every morning and evening, Jasmine took Dotty for a walk, so she could get used to the land that would be her home when she was released into the wild.

Jasmine didn't like to think too much about this. She had read a lot about roe deer, and she was horrified by how many were hit by cars, caught in fences or killed by dogs.

"Do we really have to release her?" she asked Nadia. "She's so attached to me, she's more like a dog really. She wouldn't be any trouble."

Nadia shook her head. "She's just a baby now, Jasmine, but she'll be completely different in a few months' time. It wouldn't be right to keep her once she's fully grown. Wild animals need freedom."

"I know," said Jasmine. "But it's so dangerous for deer in the wild. Imagine if something terrible happened to her and there was no one there to help her."

"Try not to imagine it," said Nadia. "Just imagine her having a lovely time instead."

Chapter Seven
Where Did She Go?

At two weeks old, Dotty was able to lap milk from a bowl, so Dad could feed her at lunchtime. She also started to nibble at soil and plants. Dandelions and chickweed were her favourites, and she loved chopped fruit and vegetables too.

Mira phoned to see how they were getting on. "I'd stop using the lead when you walk her now," she advised. "Try to behave as much like her real mother as possible. But she will start running away as she gets older, so you need to learn to call her back by whistling like her mother would."

Jasmine searched online for the sound of a roe deer calling to her fawn, and she and Tom practised the whistle until they could do it perfectly.

Tom lived on the lane that bordered Jasmine's farm, and he often joined them on their walks. But Jasmine didn't let anybody else come. It was important that Dotty kept her animal instincts and stayed wary of humans and dogs. If they saw a person or a dog on their walks, they would run away from them together, like a doe and her fawn would.

By the time she was three weeks old, Dotty was surprisingly fast at running and amazingly good at hiding. She could disappear in seconds, her coat blending in perfectly with her surroundings.

"It's lucky she always comes back when I whistle," said Jasmine. "Otherwise I don't think we'd ever find her."

It was a Sunday evening, and they were

walking Dotty around the wildflower meadow
at the northern edge of Oak Tree Farm. The
grass here was long and thick, almost ready to
be made into hay. At the top end, the meadow
bordered the woods.

"There's Ella and Sky, look," said Tom.

Two fields below them, Ella was walking along
the hedgerow towards the farmyard. Sky was
bounding through the middle of the field.

"I thought she'd stopped walking Sky now,"
said Tom.

"She has, mostly," said Jasmine, "but she said
she needed a break from revision this evening. I
didn't think she was coming up this way, though.
I thought she was going to walk along the river."

"Oh, no," said Tom, pointing to the other side
of the meadow. "Look."

A girl in shorts and a strappy top had just
climbed over the stile, while a Jack Russell
terrier ran under it. It was Bella Bradley and her
dog, Rupert. The dog that had killed the nesting

duck on the riverbank.

"Ugh," said Jasmine. "What's she doing here?"
She bent down to pick up Dotty.

Her stomach lurched. Dotty wasn't there.

"Where is she?" she asked, looking around in
panic.

"She was there a second ago," said Tom.
"Where did she go?" He stood on tiptoe and
scanned the field.

Jasmine whistled. "Dotty!" she called, and
whistled again.

There was no answering squeak. The grasses
rustled. Was that just the evening breeze, or was it
Dotty running through the tall grass? What if it
was Bella's dog chasing Dotty?

"Call your dog, Bella!" shouted Jasmine. "Put it
on a lead!"

But Bella either didn't hear or didn't take any
notice.

"I'll go and tell her," said Tom. "Keep
whistling."

He ran across the field, while Jasmine revolved
on the spot, whistling and calling. Dotty could
have run off in any direction, and she was so
good at hiding that she was almost impossible
to find. But she always came back when Jasmine
called her. Why didn't she come now?

From some distance away, Jasmine heard Ella calling Sky.

Oh, no. Two dogs on the loose!

She whistled again, desperate now. She heard Tom calling to Bella, and Ella calling Sky again. She walked across the field, whistling constantly, but Dotty was nowhere to be seen.

"Why should I?" she heard Bella say. "There's no animals in this field. Rupert can go where he likes."

"Because Jasmine's fawn has disappeared," said Tom, "and dogs attack fawns."

"That's not my problem," said Bella. "She should look after her fawn better."

"Just call him, will you?" said Tom, his voice rising in anger. "You don't want him to kill Dotty, do you?"

Jasmine heard a swishing in the grass. Rupert raced past her, barking with excitement. Her stomach clenched in horror. She was about to storm over and shout at Bella when she saw a

flash of black and white. Sky was streaking up
the field towards the wood.

"Sky!" called Ella. "Come back!"

"Sky!" called Jasmine. "Come here!"

But Sky, who was normally so obedient to
Jasmine, totally ignored her. Reaching the
top of the meadow, he leapt over the fence
into the wood. Jasmine heard the crackling of
undergrowth and a volley of sharp barks. What
was he doing?

"Rupert!" called Bella. Finally!

Tom sprinted back across the meadow. Ella
came running through the gateway from the
field below, her eyes wide with panic.

Sky ran up to Jasmine and sat at her feet,
licking her hand adoringly.

"Oh, there you are," panted Ella. "Naughty
dog. Why did you run off like that?"

She bent down and clipped his lead on. When
she straightened up again, she looked at Tom and
Jasmine and frowned.

"What's wrong?" Then she looked down at
Jasmine's feet. "Where's Dotty?"

"She's disappeared," said Jasmine despairingly.
"She just … disappeared. One minute she was
there and the next she just wasn't."

"She can't have gone far," said Ella. "I'll help
you look."

"No," said Jasmine. "You need to take Sky
home. Dotty won't come out if there are dogs
nearby."

"Wait," said Ella, looking alarmed. "You don't
think… Sky wouldn't have chased Dotty, would
he?"

"Of course he wouldn't," said Jasmine hotly.
"Sky wouldn't do anything like that. But Dotty's
instinct is to avoid dogs, so she'll hide until she
knows she's safe to come out."

"OK," said Ella, but she still looked worried.
"I hope you find her soon. Come on, Sky. We're
going home."

Chapter Eight
A Little High-Pitched Squeak

Jasmine's stomach was a mass of knots. She looked across the field and saw Bella heading back towards the lane, with Rupert on his lead again.

"Phew," said Tom. "Both dogs gone. Dotty should come when we call her now."

"Unless that horrible dog attacked her," said Jasmine. "Or frightened her so much she's run for miles. Or scared her to death," she added with a shudder.

"I bet she's just been lying still in the long

grass, waiting for the dogs to leave," said Tom. "Come on. I'll search this side of the field and you do that side."

They set off, both of them whistling to Dotty as they walked. Jasmine strained her ears for the sound of Dotty's answering call. Her heart leapt at every high-pitched squeak she heard, only to sink when she heard it again and realised it was a bird.

By the time she and Tom met at the hedge on the other side of the meadow, Jasmine was close to tears. Tom looked really worried too.

"I don't think she's in this field," he said. "She'd definitely have come back by now."

"Unless she's…" began Jasmine. But she couldn't bear to finish the sentence.

"The dogs both came from that direction," Tom said, pointing towards the farmyard. "So maybe Dotty ran into the wood to get away from them."

Jasmine's heart sank even further. "How will

we ever find her in there?"

"We'll just have to keep walking and calling and looking," said Tom. "At least it will be light for another couple of hours."

And then what? thought Jasmine. But she kept her gloomy thoughts to herself and followed Tom into the wood.

The woodland floor was covered in bracken and brambles. Jasmine and Tom were wearing shorts, so their legs were soon criss-crossed with scratches and dotted with stings. Doggedly they walked deeper into the wood, several metres apart, their eyes constantly scanning the undergrowth as they whistled.

And then Jasmine heard something. A little high-pitched squeak.

She froze, hardly daring to believe her ears. Could that be Dotty, or was it just a bird again?

Tom was rustling through the undergrowth. Jasmine called to him as quietly as she could. He turned and she put her finger to her lips.

83

He stood completely still. Jasmine whistled.

And there it was again. That tiny high-pitched squeak. Jasmine's heart leapt with joy and her face broke into an enormous smile. She looked at Tom and saw that he was grinning too.

"Where's it coming from?" he mouthed.

Jasmine whistled again. She frowned in concentration as she listened to the answering squeak. Then she pointed back to the edge of the wood.

"I think she's over there," she said.

They made their way towards the sound, their eyes scanning every inch of the ground.

Jasmine's stomach flipped as she saw a patch of speckled brown and white nestled in the roots of a tree. She hurried over to it, only to find a pile of dead leaves.

Fear gripped her heart. Why wasn't Dotty running towards her? What had happened to her?

She whistled again. The answering squeak was

very close now. Jasmine climbed over a fallen
tree trunk that lay near the fence at the edge of
the wood.

She gasped in delight. There was the little deer,
curled up in a patch of brambles,
her bright eyes gazing
straight at Jasmine.

"Oh, Dotty! You're
here!"

As Jasmine ran
towards her, Dotty
squeaked and
scrabbled about,
trying to stand up.

Why couldn't
she stand? What had
happened to her?

Jasmine knelt beside the fawn,
ignoring the thorns that pierced her knees.
Dotty was trembling and shivering, and her
heartbeat was very fast.

"Oh, Dotty, are you OK? What happened? It's all right, I'm here. You're safe now."

She continued to speak reassuringly, stroking Dotty and examining her anxiously. She couldn't see anything wrong with her. But now the fawn tried to heave herself to her feet again, and again she sank back on the ground with a squeak. There was definitely something wrong. But what?

Very gently, Jasmine took hold of the little deer around her middle and lifted her to her feet. Tom was standing on Dotty's other side. He gasped.

"What?" asked Jasmine.

"Look!" said Tom.

Jasmine turned the fawn around, and as she saw it she cried out. Blood was pouring from a gaping wound near the top of her right hind leg.

"Oh, no!" cried Jasmine. "Oh, Dotty!"

Gingerly, so as not to cause the fawn any more pain than necessary, Jasmine lifted her up. Tom took off his jumper and tucked it around her.

"Let's get her home," said Jasmine. "Mum needs to treat her."

"What if she's out?" asked Tom.

"She's not on call this weekend. She should be home. Can you phone and tell her what's happened? Then she can get everything ready."

Chapter Nine
Will She Be All Right?

Mum was waiting in the scullery. She looked tense and anxious.

"Lay her down there so I can examine her," she said, indicating the towel spread out on the work surface.

Tom helped Jasmine to lie the little fawn down. Dotty lay completely still and quiet, her big eyes open wide.

Mum sucked in her breath as she saw the wound. "That's a nasty bite," she said.

"A bite?" said Jasmine. "From a dog?"

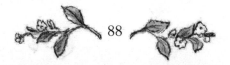

"It looks like it," said Nadia. "I'll give her an antibiotic shot first, and then we'll clean it up."

Fury surged through Jasmine. Bella's dog had done this!

She was about to let out a torrent of anger, but then she stopped herself. Dotty was suffering from pain and shock. She needed Jasmine to be calm and comforting, not tense and angry.

So Jasmine didn't let herself think about what might have caused the injury. Instead, she stroked the little fawn, looking into her wide-open eyes and murmuring comforting words, while Mum fetched the bottle of antibiotic, took a fresh syringe out of its packaging and injected Dotty at the top of her other hind leg, beside the tail. Dotty didn't react as the antibiotic went in, but she was still cold and trembling and her heartbeat felt much too fast.

"Will she be all right?" asked Jasmine, trying to stop herself from panicking. Animals could die of shock, especially small prey animals.

"I'm sure she will be," said Mum, but she didn't sound convincing. "I'm going to give her a painkiller and then we'll clean up the wound. Can you fetch my clippers, please? And can you put some antiseptic in a bowl, and get the cotton wool balls too."

She gave Dotty an injection of painkiller while Jasmine poured some pink antiseptic liquid into a plastic bowl. She brought it to her mum with the bag of cotton wool balls. Tom fetched the clippers and handed them to Nadia.

"That's a deep wound," said Nadia, as she shaved off the fur around the bite. "It's gone right through to the bone."

Jasmine peered at the gaping hole and gasped when she saw the white bone beneath the flesh.

"Will it heal?" asked Tom. "Will her leg be OK?"

"I can't say yet," said Nadia. "We'll just have to do the best we can."

"What does that mean?" asked Jasmine, her

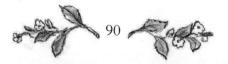

voice rising in alarm. "Do you mean she might lose her leg?"

"Let's hope it doesn't come to that," said Nadia.

She dipped a cotton wool ball into the liquid and began to clean the wound, using a fresh ball for each stroke. Once the wound was completely clean, she started to feel carefully along Dotty's leg. When she got to the thin part below the knee, she stopped and frowned.

"What's wrong?" asked Jasmine.

"I'm afraid her bone's broken," Mum said. "Quite badly broken, by the feel of it."

"Oh, no!" said Jasmine. "Oh, poor Dotty!"

"She was next to the fence when we found her," said Tom. "Maybe she tried to jump over it and hit her leg on a bar."

"She could well have done," said Mum. She was still feeling gently round the leg, just above the hoof. Tom and Jasmine waited anxiously.

Eventually, Mum straightened up and looked

at Jasmine. "I'm going to take her into the surgery," she said.

Jasmine turned cold with fear. "What are you going to do?" she asked. Her voice came out squeaky with panic.

"I need to give her an X-ray," said Mum. "And then we'll see what has to be done."

At the surgery, Jasmine carried Dotty's cage into the treatment room, where Mum laid her carefully on the table. Linda, the head nurse, came in to assist her.

"I need you two to leave the room while we do the X-ray," Nadia said to the children. "It's standard practice," she explained to Tom. "So you're not exposed to radiation."

Tom and Jasmine hovered anxiously outside the door. They didn't speak, or even look at each other. They just waited.

Eventually, Linda called them back in. Dotty was lying motionless on the table. Nadia was

standing at her computer screen, which showed a black-and-white image. She turned to look at the children.

"Here's the X-ray of her leg," she said. "You can see how badly broken it is below the knee."

Jasmine looked in silent misery at the picture of the shattered bone.

"And also," said Nadia, bringing up another image, "the force of the bite has fractured her thigh bone too."

Jasmine's throat tightened painfully. She couldn't speak.

It was Tom who asked the question.

"What's going to happen to her?"

Mum looked at them seriously before she spoke.

"There's only one thing we can do, I'm afraid. If we're going to have any chance of saving her life, we need to amputate the leg."

Chapter Ten
You Just Wait

Jasmine's heart felt sick and heavy. Her head hurt with the effort of trying not to picture what Dotty was about to go through. She was furious with herself. This was all her fault. How had she lost sight of her like that? How could she have been so careless?

Nadia insisted that Jasmine and Tom went home while she performed the surgery.

"There's no point in you staying," she said when Jasmine protested. "She'll be under general anaesthetic, so she'll be asleep the whole time.

And you've got school in the morning. You need to get some rest."

Dad came to collect them. Nobody said much on the way home, but during the journey Jasmine's guilt and misery gradually turned to rage.

"Do you have any idea how it happened?" Dad asked as they walked into the kitchen.

"It was Bella Bradley and her horrible dog," Jasmine said. "He was off the lead in the field where we were walking Dotty. Tom told her to put him on a lead and she just argued, and then I saw him running towards the wood, barking and barking, and then we found Dotty with that awful bite. You need to phone the police, Dad. Phone them right now."

"Did you actually see Bella's dog attack Dotty?" asked Dad.

"No, but it was obviously him."

"Did you see any other animals around?" asked Dad. "A fox, or any other dogs?"

"Well," said Tom, glancing nervously at Jasmine. "Ella was walking Sky, and he was off the lead too."

Dad frowned. "Sky was there?"

"That's nothing to do with it," said Jasmine. "Sky would never hurt Dotty."

"What?" said a voice behind them. "What about Sky and Dotty?"

They all looked round. Jasmine hadn't heard Ella come into the kitchen.

In the awkward silence that followed, Ella said, "What's happened? Where's Dotty?"

A lump came into Jasmine's throat. Tom looked at the ground.

"Dotty was bitten while Tom and Jasmine were walking her," said Dad.

Ella looked horror-stricken. "Bitten? By Sky?"

"No!" said Jasmine. "Sky would never do that. He's never attacked anyone."

"He bit you once," said Dad.

"When he was terrified! He wasn't frightened

97

today, was he? And we know Bella's dog's a murderer. We saw him kill a duck for no reason at all. He just likes killing. He should be put down. You need to call the police, Dad."

"Killing?" cried Ella. "What do you mean? Where's Dotty?"

"She's at the surgery," said Dad. "Her leg was badly damaged. Mum's having to amputate it, I'm afraid."

"No!" wailed Ella. "Oh, no, poor Dotty!"

"I'm sure she'll be all right," said Dad. "Mum's a brilliant surgeon, and there are plenty of deer who've lost a leg and manage with three."

"But it's all my fault," said Ella. "I didn't have Sky under control. I killed Dotty's mother and now I've hurt Dotty."

And she burst into tears and ran from the room.

"That's all we need," said Dad. "She's only just recovering from last time."

"It wasn't anything to do with her," said

98

Jasmine. "I don't know why you didn't tell her that. It was obviously Bella's dog."

"Jasmine, you can't go around accusing people's dogs without any evidence," said Dad.

Jasmine stared at him in outrage. "So you're just going to let Bella and her horrible dog get away with this? You're going to do nothing and let him go around killing as many animals as he wants to?"

"Jasmine, calm down," said Dad.

"No!" shouted Jasmine. "I won't calm down! And if you won't do anything about it, then I will. You wait until I see Bella Bradley in the morning. I'll tell her exactly what her horrible dog did, and then I'll report her to the police. And you can't stop me."

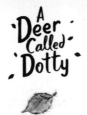

Mum phoned as soon as the operation was over.

"It all went well," she told Jasmine. "Dotty's still asleep from the anaesthetic, so she'll stay at the surgery overnight. We've moved her into a comfortable cage, and Linda's on night duty, so she'll be keeping watch over her."

Jasmine lay awake for hours that night, far too worried and angry to go to sleep. As soon as she woke on Monday morning, all the previous night's emotions flooded back into her head. She scrambled out of bed and ran downstairs.

Nadia looked up from her cup of tea as Jasmine walked into the kitchen. "Linda just phoned," she said. "Dotty's woken up, and she seems well and comfortable."

"Can we go and see her now?"

"No," said Mum. "There's no time before school. I'll bring her home after work. Don't worry, she'll be well looked after. The nurses will dote on her."

Jasmine could tell there was no point arguing. She went to fetch the cereal from the cupboard.

"Oh, and, Jasmine?" said Mum.

"Yes?"

"Don't do anything silly at school, will you? You have no proof that it was Bella's dog that attacked Dotty. It sounds as though it could just as easily have been Sky. So don't go accusing Bella of anything, will you?"

Jasmine didn't reply. There was no way she was going to let Bella get away with this.

You just wait, Bella Bradley, she thought. *You just wait.*

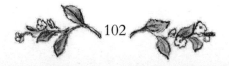

Chapter Eleven
I Can't Apologise

Jasmine arrived in the playground just before school started. She spotted Bella immediately, chatting and laughing with a group of other girls. Jasmine strode towards her. She was vaguely aware that Tom was trying to say something, but she didn't hear the words. Nothing existed in her world right then except her boiling rage, her injured fawn and Bella's smug face.

One of Bella's friends nudged her as Jasmine drew near. Bella turned, and she and Jasmine stood face to face.

103

"How dare you!" shouted Jasmine. "How dare you let your dog loose to attack my fawn?"

"Don't accuse my dog of stuff he didn't do," said Bella. "I could see him all the time. He didn't go anywhere near your stupid fawn."

"Liar!" shouted Jasmine. "Liar and murderer! You let your dog kill that duck and now you let him almost kill my fawn. Dotty's lost her leg because of him and you don't care one bit. He could have killed her and you still wouldn't care. You're a horrible person and I hate you! I hate you so much! I'm going to call the police and they'll come and arrest you and have your dog put down, and it will serve you right because you're evil!"

Bella stood wide-eyed and open-mouthed in shock. Jasmine suddenly realised that the entire playground had gone silent. The teachers had come out to lead their classes into school, and every single teacher was staring at her.

As the world reshaped itself around her, Jasmine saw the head teacher detach herself from the horrified group of staff and stride purposefully and fatefully towards her.

"Come with me, please," she said to Jasmine and Bella. "To my office. Now."

Jasmine sat in the head teacher's office, her mouth stubbornly closed. Why could nobody else in the world see the blindingly obvious truth? Of course it had been Bella's dog that had attacked Dotty. Anyone with half a brain could have worked that out. And yet here was Mrs Allerton, just like her own parents, saying there was no actual evidence.

Bella had been interviewed separately, so

Jasmine didn't know exactly what she'd said, but it wasn't hard to guess. Of course she would say her dog hadn't done it, but why would anyone believe Bella's word against hers?

It was never a good idea to argue with Mrs Allerton, though. So, once Jasmine had stated her case as forcefully as she could, she kept her mouth shut and let the head teacher speak.

But then Mrs Allerton said, "You need to apologise to Bella."

"What!" exclaimed Jasmine. "No!"

"Yes."

Jasmine shook her head. "Never. I'm not apologising to her. I meant everything I said. She *is* evil and so is her dog."

Mrs Allerton held up her hand for silence. "I'm going to give you a minute to reconsider your decision, Jasmine, before I phone your parents. Just sit there and have a good think."

She picked up a letter from her desk and began to read it. Jasmine sat with her arms

crossed, looking out of the window at the trees in the playground. If Mrs Allerton thought she was going to change her mind, she had another think coming.

"Well?" said the head, after a silence that seemed to have lasted far longer than a minute.

Jasmine's stomach squirmed, but she shook her head again. "I can't apologise to Bella."

Mrs Allerton gave a heavy sigh. She tapped a few keys on her computer keyboard and then she picked up the phone and dialled a number.

Jasmine hoped she was dialling the home number. Neither of her parents would be in to answer the phone. But Mrs Allerton had clearly called Nadia's mobile, because within a few rings she said, "Oh, hello, Mrs Green."

Jasmine listened with a heavy heart as the head teacher relayed their conversation. She knew better than to expect sympathy from her mother.

When Mrs Allerton had finished explaining, there was a long silence as she listened to Nadia's

reply. Jasmine strained to hear, but she couldn't make out the words. All she could hear was the head teacher saying things like, "Oh, I see," and "How interesting."

What could Mum possibly be saying that took that long and was that interesting?

Then Mrs Allerton said, "Yes, I think that would be a very good idea." There was a pause and then she said, "That will be fine. Twelve o'clock then. Thank you."

She put the phone down and looked at Jasmine.

"Your mother is coming into school at lunchtime," she said. "Until then, you can work in the corner of my office. I don't think it would be a good idea for you to return to your classroom."

Chapter Twelve
New Information

Jasmine spent the rest of the morning at a little table in the corner of the head teacher's office. It was impossible to concentrate on the worksheets in front of her. Was she going to be expelled? Why else would Mum be leaving work in the middle of the day to come to the school?

They wouldn't really expel her for this, would they? But they might suspend her. Oh, Mum and Dad were going to be so mad.

She checked the clock again. Five past eleven. Surely this clock was slower than every other

clock in the world. Never had a morning
dragged on so long.

On the dot of twelve o'clock, there was a
knock at the door. Jasmine didn't turn round, but
she heard the door open and the school secretary
say, "Mrs Green's here to see you, Jill."

"Thank you," said Mrs Allerton. "Show her in,
please. Jasmine, you'd better come and sit over
here."

Jasmine felt sick as she sat down opposite the
head teacher's desk. When her mum walked in,
she didn't dare look up. She could imagine her
fury at being called away from work to deal with
this.

The room was so hot. Why weren't the
windows open?

Mrs Allerton greeted Nadia and asked her to
take a seat beside Jasmine.

"Your mother has kindly taken the time to
come here," she said, "because she's found out
some new information about what happened to

your fawn, and we thought it would be good if you knew as soon as possible."

Jasmine stared at her mother. New information?

"Would you like to tell us what you know, Mrs Green?" said Mrs Allerton.

"Thank you," said Mum. "I had a phone call this morning from a retired man who lives in the village. He was flying a drone over the woods yesterday evening, and this morning he looked through the footage on his TV, to see it more clearly. And he noticed something he hadn't seen before."

She paused.

"What did he notice?" asked Jasmine, unable to contain herself.

"He saw a roe deer fawn being chased into the woods and attacked," said Nadia.

"I knew it!" said Jasmine. "I told you it was her dog, didn't I? She can apologise to me now."

"It wasn't Bella's dog," said Nadia.

Jasmine's heart felt as though it was being

112

gripped in a vice. Not Sky? It couldn't have been Sky. *Please don't let it have been Sky*, she thought.

"It wasn't a dog that attacked Dotty," said Mum.

Jasmine stared at her, unable to take this in. Then sheer relief flooded through her body. It wasn't Sky!

"It was a fox," said Mum. "A big hungry-looking fox. I've seen the footage."

"Oh, poor Dotty!" said Jasmine, shuddering as she saw in her mind's eye a horribly vivid picture of the little fawn being set upon by a huge hungry fox.

Then she frowned in puzzlement. A three-week-old fawn would never be able to fight off a fox.

"How did she get away?" she asked.

Mum smiled. "That's the amazing thing. Sky saved her."

"Sky? How?"

"You saw Sky run into the wood, didn't you?

And you heard him barking. He was chasing the fox away, Jasmine. Sky saw off the fox, and then he ran back to you. It's all in the film footage."

Jasmine gazed at her mother in astonishment and growing delight as these extraordinary facts sank in. Sky wasn't the attacker. He was a hero!

"I phoned Ella straightaway," said Mum. "She was so relieved she was in tears, poor thing. I'm so pleased for her. She's been miserable."

Jasmine was filled with an overwhelming happiness. Everything was all right again.

And then the head teacher spoke and brought her straight back down to earth.

"So, Jasmine," she said, "I think you'll agree now that you owe Bella an apology. I'll see your mum out and then we'll talk."

Nadia gave Jasmine a very stern look. "Make sure you apologise properly to Bella," she said. "I'm not at all happy with your behaviour."

Mrs Allerton showed Mum out of the room, thanking her for giving up her time to come

into school.

"Not at all," said Mum. "I'm very sorry that my daughter has taken up so much of your day."

Jasmine strained to hear the reply, but they were too far away by then and there was a lot of lunchtime noise in the corridor. After a couple of minutes, the door opened again and Mrs Allerton reappeared. Behind her was Bella Bradley.

"Sit down, Bella," said the head teacher, indicating the chair where Mum had sat.

Bella perched on the edge of the chair, her back very straight. She didn't look at Jasmine. Jasmine didn't look at her.

"Jasmine," said Mrs Allerton, "do you have something to say to Bella?"

Jasmine took a deep breath. She kept her eyes on the head teacher's desk.

"It wasn't your dog that attacked Dotty," she said.

"I knew it!" said Bella. "It was your dog all

116

along. I told you!"

"It was not my dog," said Jasmine. "It was a fox. My dog saw off the fox and saved Dotty."

"I told you it wasn't Rupert," said Bella. "I said I could see him all the time."

"Yes," said Jasmine.

Silence.

Mrs Allerton turned to Jasmine.

"Don't you have anything else to say, Jasmine?"

Jasmine was hoping she had said enough. But clearly it wasn't enough to satisfy the head teacher.

"I'm sorry I shouted at you," she said. "I didn't mean it."

Bella looked directly at her for the first time. "You did mean it," she said. "You totally meant it."

Jasmine was taken aback. Bella was right. She had meant it. She had called Bella evil. She had called her dog evil. She had threatened to call the police and have Bella's dog put down. She had screamed at Bella in front of the whole school. And she had refused to listen when literally everybody had told her she was being unreasonable.

How would she have felt if Bella had said those things about her and Sky? She would have gone crazy. Looking at Bella now, sitting quietly opposite her, she felt a grudging respect. There was no way she could have behaved with that

118

sort of dignity if their places had been switched.

She took another deep breath.

"You're right," she said. "I did mean it at the time. I'm sorry. I was really worried about Dotty."

She stopped. She knew that wasn't the whole truth. She had been worried about Dotty, of course, but would she have reacted quite so violently if it had been anybody else's dog in that field?

"And I don't like you or your dog, so I was really angry."

Mrs Allerton's eyebrows shot up into her fringe.

"I don't like you either," said Bella. "Your dog's all right, though."

"Thanks," said Jasmine.

The corner of Mrs Allerton's mouth twitched slightly. "Well," she said. "That was an apology of sorts, I suppose. I think we've established that you're never going to be best friends, but I

would really appreciate it if you could make it through the rest of the year without any more arguments. Civil behaviour, that's all I'm asking. Do you think you can manage that?"

"Yes, Mrs Allerton," they said.

"That's amazing," said Tom, when Jasmine told him the story as they walked home from school. "I can't believe Sky did that. What a hero."

"Sky would never hurt Dotty," said Jasmine. "Or any animal."

Tom glanced at her. "I didn't really think he'd hurt her. I just thought I should say he was in the field. Just so your mum and dad knew all the facts, you know?"

"I know," said Jasmine. Tom was much more reasonable and level-headed than she was. He never lost his temper or wrongly accused people.

"Ella must be so happy," said Tom.

When they walked into the farmhouse, Ella was sitting at the kitchen table, drinking tea and eating toast. Sky sat proudly beside her, and both of them looked perfectly contented. Sky got up and trotted towards Jasmine, wagging his tail. Jasmine threw her arms around him.

"Sky saved Dotty!" said Ella. "He was a hero."

"He's the best dog ever," said Jasmine, hugging him tightly. Sky licked her left ear.

"If he hadn't been there, and he hadn't been off the lead," said Ella, "then poor little Dotty..." She shuddered.

"You saved her life," said Jasmine. "You and Sky."

And she kissed Sky's head and buried her face in his long silky coat.

Chapter Thirteen
Dotty Comes Home

At five o'clock, as Jasmine was feeding the cats in the scullery, the back door opened and Nadia appeared, carrying the puppy crate.

"Oh!" cried Jasmine. "She's home!"

"She's home," said Nadia. "And she'll be very pleased to see you."

She set the crate down and Jasmine knelt beside it, smiling at the little fawn curled up on the cage floor. Dotty squeaked in greeting.

"Hello, Dotty," said Jasmine, unfastening the catches. "It's so lovely to see you again."

She opened the door and Dotty licked her hand. Then, to Jasmine's amazement, she struggled to her feet and stumbled out of the crate. She nuzzled into Jasmine's neck and started to lick her face.

"You're walking!" exclaimed Jasmine. "You clever girl!"

She gathered the little fawn into her arms and hugged her, careful not to touch the bandaged stump where Dotty's leg had been.

"That's the first time she's stood up," said Nadia. "She must have wanted to walk for you."

Jasmine kissed Dotty's shiny black nose. "You're amazing," she said. "I can't believe you're already walking, after everything that's happened to you."

She set the fawn on the floor, curious to see how well she could walk. Dotty hobbled across the tiles to where Toffee was sitting. She started to lick Toffee's face. Toffee began to purr.

Nadia's eyes widened in surprise. "Wow," she

said. "She's really pleased to be home."

"Oh, Dotty," said Jasmine. "It's so good to have you back."

Over the next week, Dotty grew stronger and stronger. Jasmine spent every moment she

could with her, building up her strength and confidence. Each morning and evening they went for walks around the garden, with Dotty on a lead. She adapted remarkably quickly to walking on three legs. The loss of a limb didn't seem to bother her at all.

"She won't be able to live in the wild, though, will she?" said Jasmine to her mum on the following Saturday. Nadia was weeding a flower bed and Jasmine was walking Dotty around the garden. "I've been reading about deer with three legs and people say herd animals with three legs can be OK in the wild, because the group looks out for them. But it's bad for roe deer, because they mostly live alone. I'm not going to release Dotty on her own and then have her killed."

"Nobody's asking you to do that," said Nadia, uprooting a dandelion with her trowel.

Jasmine stared at her mother, her eyes wide with hope. "Really?"

"I'm sure the rescue centre over at Anslow

will take her. We're in contact with them a lot at the surgery and they're very nice. I think they've already got some three-legged deer there."

"But why can't I keep her?"

"Jasmine, you've got enough animals already. Dotty will need an enclosure with deer-proof fencing. And it will be good for her to live with other deer."

"She'd be much happier staying here. I know she would."

"You mean you would."

"We both would."

Nadia stood up and brushed the soil from her hands. "I'm not going to argue about it. I need to go and collect Manu."

Jasmine gazed at her mother's back as she made her way up the path. How could she persuade her that Dotty had to stay?

She was standing by the orchard fence pondering this question when Tom arrived half an hour later.

"What's wrong?" he asked. "You look sad."

Jasmine told him what Nadia had said about the rescue centre.

"I couldn't bear it if she had to go," she said. "But I don't know what to do. You can't exactly keep a deer in secret. She needs a big outdoor place with high fences, and—"

She stopped and stared into the orchard, where Truffle and Bramble lay dozing under an apple tree.

"I've got an idea," she said.

127

"What?"

"Come and see. Come on, Dotty."

She unbolted the gate that led into the orchard. It was a big orchard, surrounded by a high fence. A fence that was definitely deer-proof.

Jasmine shut the gate behind them. Dotty sniffed at the long grass.

"Bramble!" called Jasmine.

Bramble's ears pricked and she raised her head enquiringly. Then she got to her feet and trotted towards Jasmine, wagging her tail.

Jasmine had been so careful to keep Dotty away from dogs that this felt very strange. But everything was different now, and it was surely worth a try.

"Sit, Bramble," said Jasmine.

Bramble sat, looking expectantly at Jasmine. Dotty stared at the spaniel. Then she stretched out her long neck and licked Bramble's face.

Jasmine held her breath and clasped Dotty's

128

lead tightly in case Bramble snapped.

But Bramble didn't snap. She sat perfectly still, as though waiting to see what this strange new creature might do next.

Dotty licked the spaniel's face again. Bramble turned her head to look at her. Dotty started to nuzzle her coat, nibbling very gently at the fur on her neck.

The old spaniel got to her feet. Jasmine tensed.

Bramble started to sniff Dotty's neck. Then she sniffed along her back. Tom and Jasmine watched, motionless, as the two animals explored each other's scents.

Then Bramble put out her long pink tongue and started to lick the side of Dotty's face, around the corners of her mouth. Dotty nuzzled in closer.

Tom and Jasmine grinned at each other. They were bonding!

They watched for a while in silence as the two animals groomed each other. It was amazing to

see the bond developing between the old spaniel and the young fawn.

"Imagine if people did that," said Jasmine. "Imagine if when we met a new person we sniffed them and licked them to see if we liked them."

"Ugh," said Tom. "I'm glad we don't."

Jasmine's eye fell on a chewed-up tennis ball lying in the long grass. Suddenly she had an idea. She unclipped Dotty's lead.

"Bramble! Dotty!" she called. She held up the ball. Both animals fixed their eyes on it.

"Fetch!" called Jasmine.

She hurled the ball past where
Truffle was lying, down towards
the far end of the orchard. Bramble
immediately raced after it. The
little deer followed her new friend,
bounding through the grass on her
three legs.

"Look at that!" exclaimed Jasmine in delight. "She's running!"

Bramble snuffled about in the grass for a bit, found the ball and came running back with it in her mouth. Dotty followed her, but as she passed Truffle, she stopped. She stood completely still, staring at the enormous pig lying in the sun.

"She's never seen a pig before," said Jasmine. "She has no idea what it is."

She took the ball from Bramble and threw it again. As Bramble chased after it, Jasmine walked towards Dotty, ready to grab the fawn if Truffle decided she didn't like the look of her.

Dotty stayed frozen to the spot for a while. Then she bent her head down and sniffed Truffle's face. Truffle flapped her huge floppy ear. Startled, Dotty backed away. But after a minute she bent her head and sniffed Truffle's face again.

The pig gave a loud grunt and raised her head. Dotty froze in shock. Truffle got to her feet. Jasmine stood poised and tense.

The massive sow and the tiny fawn stood face
to face. Then Dotty leaned forward and sniffed
Truffle's snout. Truffle grunted again. Dotty
nuzzled the side of her face. Then she licked the
back of Truffle's ear.

Truffle gave the low, contented grunt that
Jasmine recognised so well. It was the same grunt
she made when Jasmine scratched her behind
the ears.

Dotty seemed to sense that Truffle was
enjoying herself. She moved closer to the huge
sow, licking and nuzzling her face as Truffle
grunted happily.

And then, to Jasmine's amazement and delight,
Truffle did what she always did when she was
completely happy. She flopped down on her side
and lay, blissfully relaxed, in the lush green grass.
Dotty backed away as the pig moved, but as soon
as she was lying down again Dotty returned to
her side and continued to lick her face.

Bramble trotted back and dropped the ball at

133

Jasmine's feet. But instead of waiting for Jasmine to throw it again, she ambled over to Dotty and sat beside her.

From the house came the sound of a window being opened, and then Ella's voice.

"Jasmine! Tom! Dinner's ready!"

Jasmine hesitated for a second. Then she said, "Wait here, Tom."

She ran into the garden and called to Ella. "Can you all come here for a minute?"

"It's dinner time," said Ella.

"Just for a minute," said Jasmine. "I need to show you something. All of you. It's important."

"OK," said Ella wearily. "I'll get them."

Jasmine waited in the garden until Ella, Manu, Mum and Dad appeared.

"Couldn't this wait?" asked Nadia.

"No," said Jasmine. "Come on. It will only take a minute, I promise."

She led them into the orchard. And there was Dotty, curled up under the apple tree, with

Truffle lying on one side of her and Bramble sitting on the other, grooming the little fawn's face with her tongue.

"Oh, my goodness!" exclaimed Nadia. "What an amazing sight!" She stared at Jasmine and Tom. "How on earth did you manage that?"

"We didn't do anything," said Jasmine. "We just brought Dotty in here and they introduced themselves and decided they liked each other."

"Is this a plot?" said Dad. "You're hoping that Mum and I will look at the three of them all cuddled up together and decide that Dotty can stay here instead of going to a rescue centre, yes?"

"Of course," said Jasmine. "Has it worked?"

Mum and Dad looked at each other. Ella, Manu, Tom and Jasmine all looked at Nadia and Michael.

"Please?" said Ella. "They look so happy together. And Dotty would have a lovely life here."

"I can take her to school for show and tell," said Manu. "No one's ever brought in a three-legged deer before."

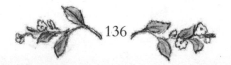

Jasmine gave her parents her most pleading
look. "Please?" she asked. "You know I'll look
after her. And she won't be any trouble living
in the orchard. You can see how settled she is
already."

Mum bent down and stroked the little fawn.
Dotty licked her hand.

"I don't really see how we can say no," she said.
"She's clearly part of the family now."

Jasmine threw her arms around her mother.
"Oh, thank you! Thank you so much! You're the
best mother ever."

"That's true," said Nadia, as Jasmine hugged her dad and thanked him too. "I am."

Jasmine gathered the little fawn in her arms and kissed her soft furry neck. "You're staying here, Dotty. This is your home now. What do you think of that?"

Dotty lifted her beautiful head and licked Jasmine's face.

"I think that means she's pleased," said Jasmine. "Welcome to the family, Dotty."

Acknowledgements

*I am hugely grateful to Chris and Sylvia Collinson,
two awe-inspiring people who have been rescuing and
rehabilitating injured and orphaned deer in the Ashdown
Forest for many years. Thank you so much for welcoming
me into your home, introducing me to your rescued fawns
and patiently answering all my questions. Any errors in the
book are, of course, entirely my own.*